Jellybean Book

Richard Scarry's
Little
ABC

Random House 🏠 New York

Copyright © 1998 by the Estate of Richard Scarry.
Copyright © 1971, 1976, 1979 by Richard Scarry.
All rights reserved. Originally published in different form
in *Richard Scarry's ABC Word Book* (1971),
Richard Scarry's Little ABC (1976), and
Richard Scarry's Best Little First Book Ever (1979).
First Random House Jellybean Books™ edition, 1998.
ISBN: 0-679-89239-7
http://www.randomhouse.com/

Printed in the United States of America
10 9 8 7 6 5 4 3 2 1

JELLYBEAN BOOKS is a trademark
of Random House, Inc.

A a

All right! Has **a**nyone seen the pilot of that **a**irplane? He could cause **a**n **a**ccident!

airplane

ants

artwork

artist

Cc

Come to the picnic!

cone

cup

You can have ice cream and cider served from a cement mixer.

cat

candles

cookies

cake

But could you please be careful and not crash into the center of the cake?

Bb

Whoever threw their **b**oot into the **b**ay from that **b**ig **b**lue ship should learn how to **b**ehave!

bow

book

broom

blouse

brush

boot

bottle

boat bottom

detour sign

D d

dump truck

dog **d**itch **d**igger

dirt

Didn't that **d**river see the **d**etour sign? He **d**rove his **d**ump truck into a **d**itch. That **d**oesn't make the **d**itch **d**igger very happy, **d**oes it?

danger sign

a **d**eep **d**itch

E e

Ernie **E**lephant
drives the fire **e**ngine
to the **e**mergency.

ear

eye

elephant

eight

eggs

empty
basket

flag

F f

fox

flower

faucet

fireplace

flames

fork

flour

floor

file

flagpole

fly

There are **f**ive **f**riendly little **f**oxes upstairs in the **F**ox **f**amily **f**armhouse.

five **f**lies

G g

Oh, no!
The **g**oats
are **g**etting
greased!

glasses

goat

globs of **g**rease

helicopter

H h

Hey! **H**ave you seen that
helicopter **h**overing near the tree?

tree **h**ouse

I i

Willy, a little **i**mp,
drips **i**ce cream
on Uncle **I**rving's
impeccably **i**roned
shirt.

ice cream

Willy the **i**mp

Uncle Irving

J j

There is lots to do
at the playground.
Jump, cat, **j**ump!

jump rope

jungle gym

K k

Kangaroo
skates by
Lowly Worm
giving Chick
a **k**iss.

kangaroo

kiss

L l

Choo! Choo! The **l**ocomotive pulls
a **l**oad of **l**ong **l**ogs.

locomotive

load of long logs

M m

A **m**otorcycle, **m**ilk truck, and **m**ail truck **m**ove **m**errily past the **m**onument.

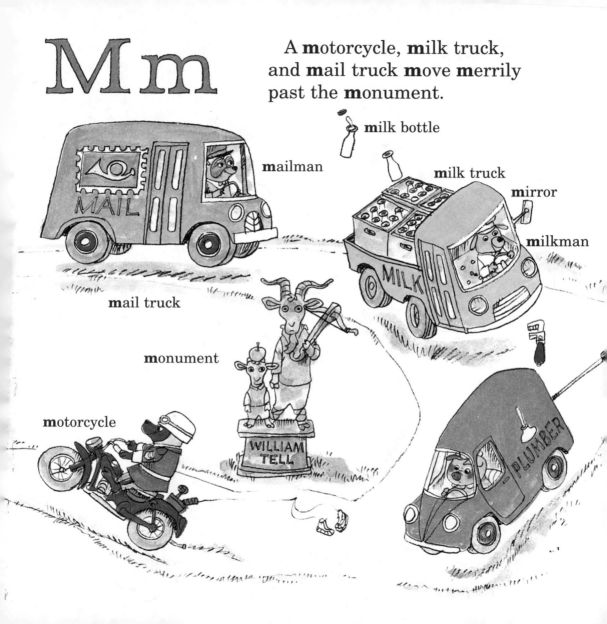

milk bottle

mailman

milk truck

mirror

milkman

mail truck

monument

motorcycle

MAIL

MILK

WILLIAM TELL

PLUMBER

N n

Not so fast, Bananas! It's very **n**aughty to steal, and **n**ow you're in trouble!

net

nurse

North Main street sign

nine pine trees

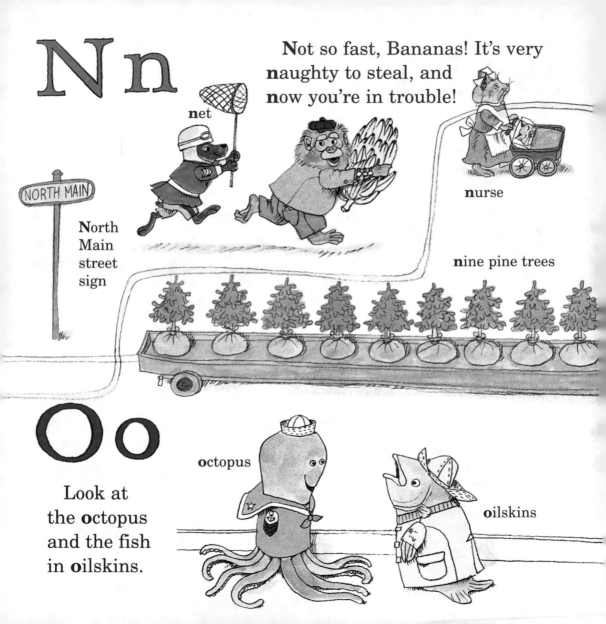

O o

Look at the **o**ctopus and the fish in **o**ilskins.

octopus

oilskins

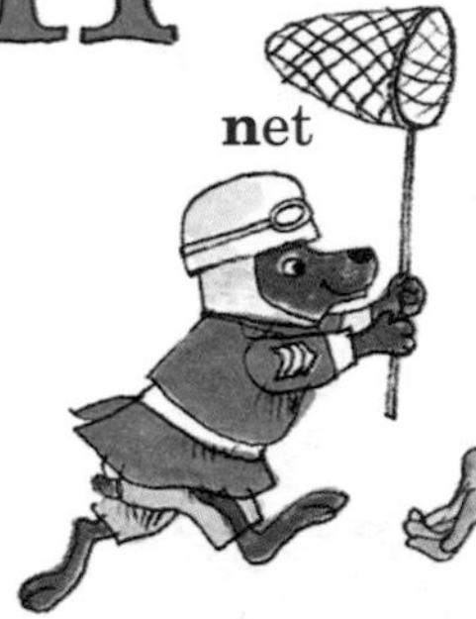

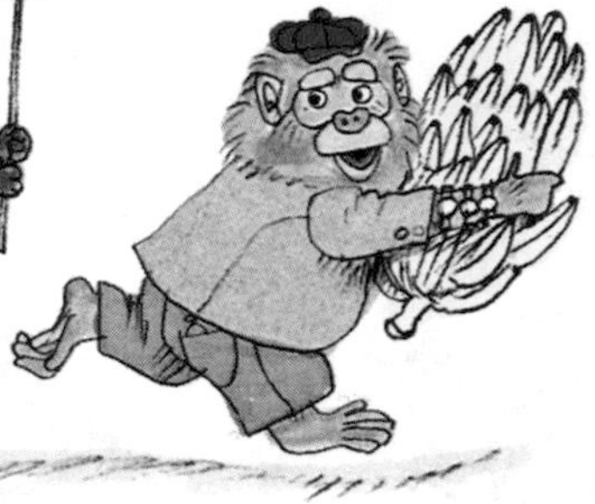

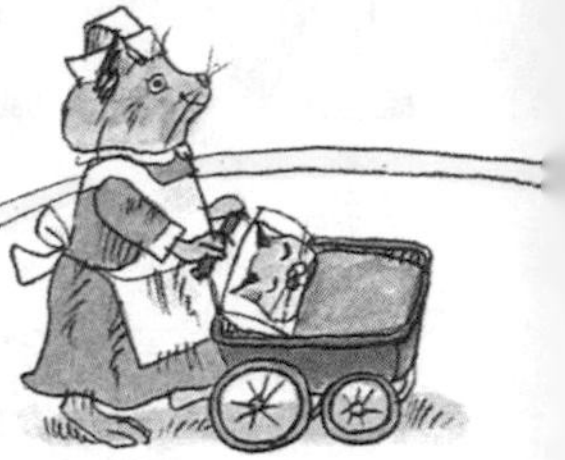

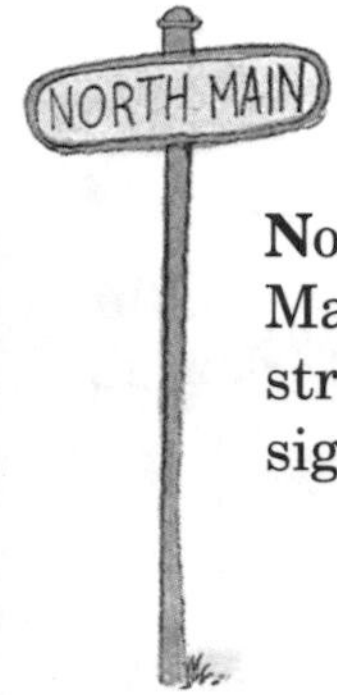

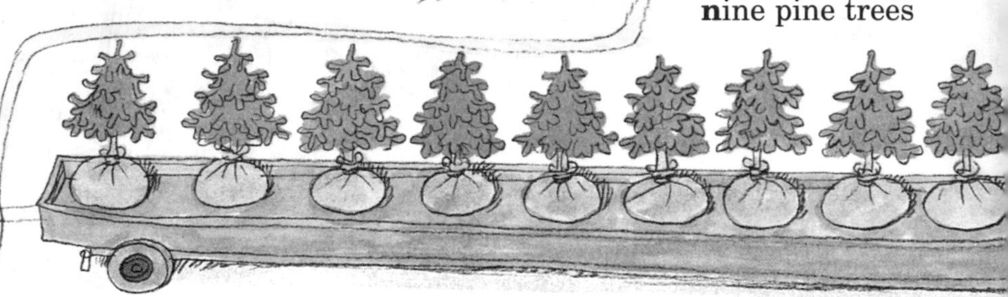

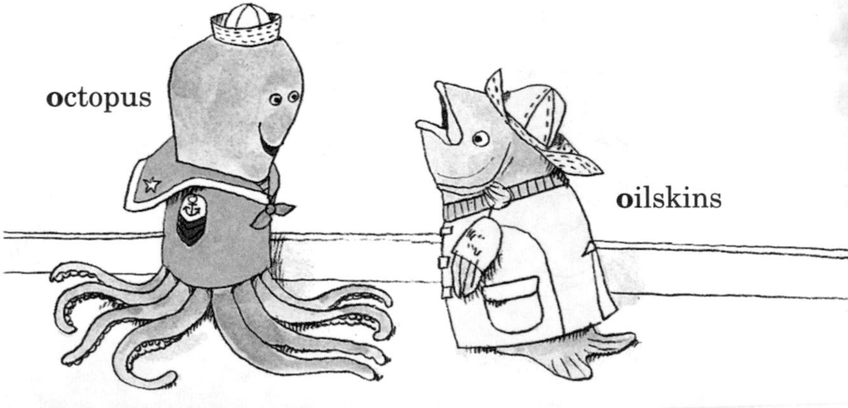

P p

Patsy Pelican is giving a **party** at her **place**. **Penguin**, **Parrot**, and **Puffin** are bringing **presents**. **Pig**, Mouse, and **Porcupine** are **playing** instruments.

plaid

pig

piccolo

porcupine

paper hat

penguin

puffin

parrot

pelican

present

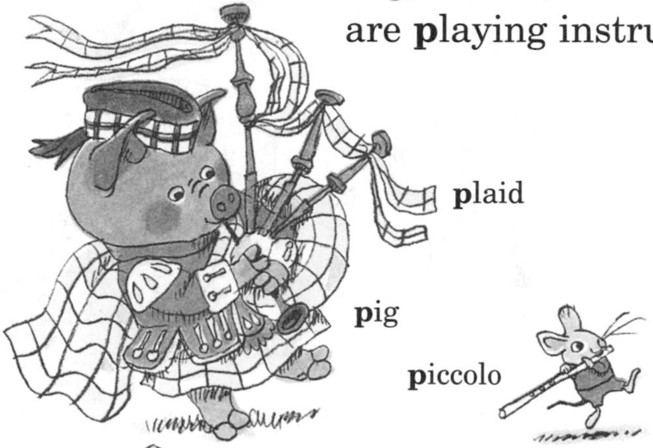

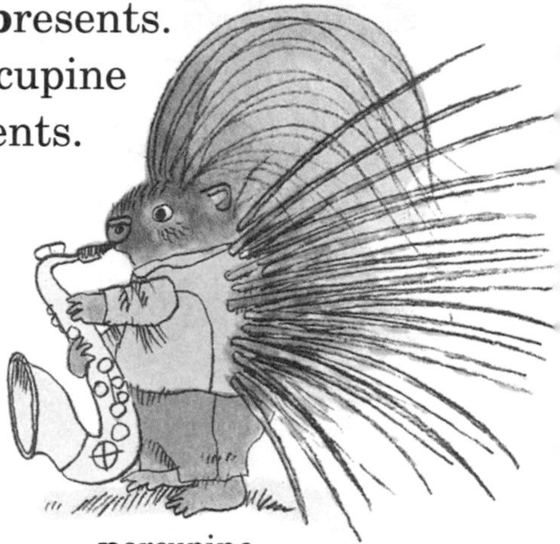

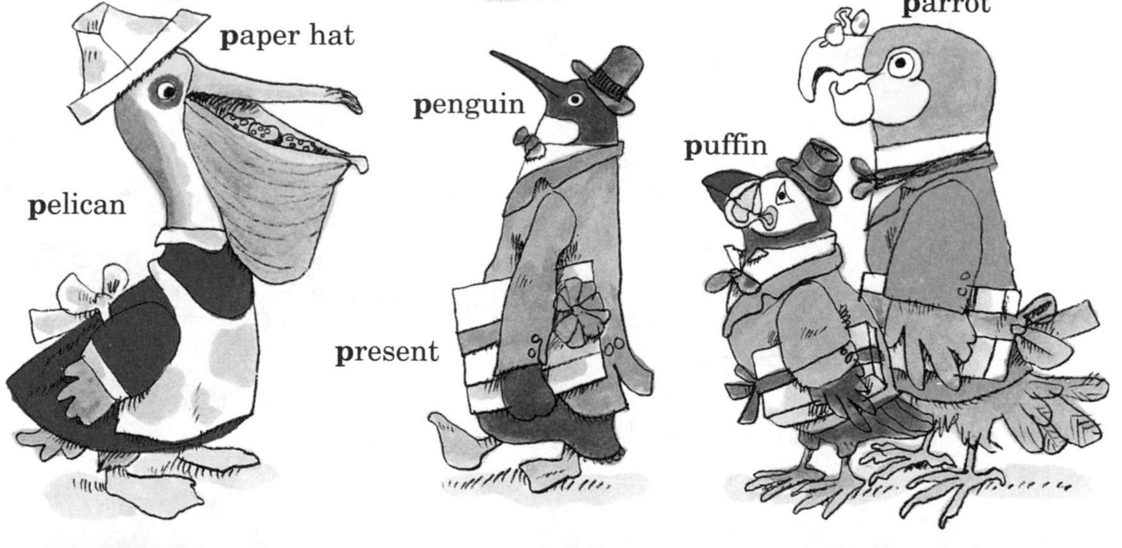

Q q

queen

It's **qu**ite all right
for a **qu**een to wear
a **qu**ilted coat when
playing croquet.

quilted coat

R r

The **r**abbits are **r**eady to **r**ow.
Row, **r**abbits, **r**ow!

ribbon

rabbits

rudder

rowboat

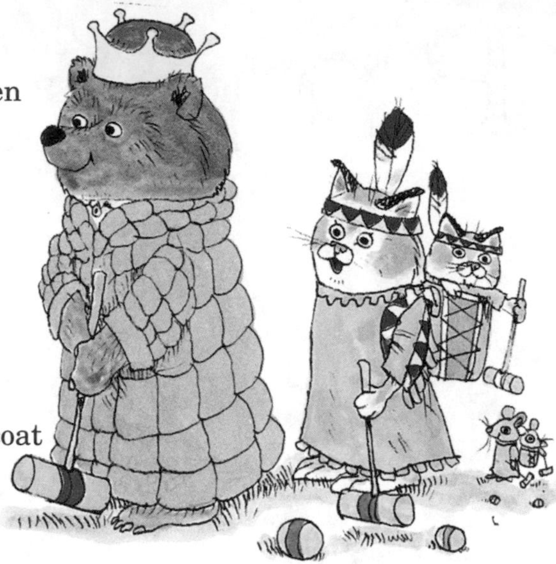

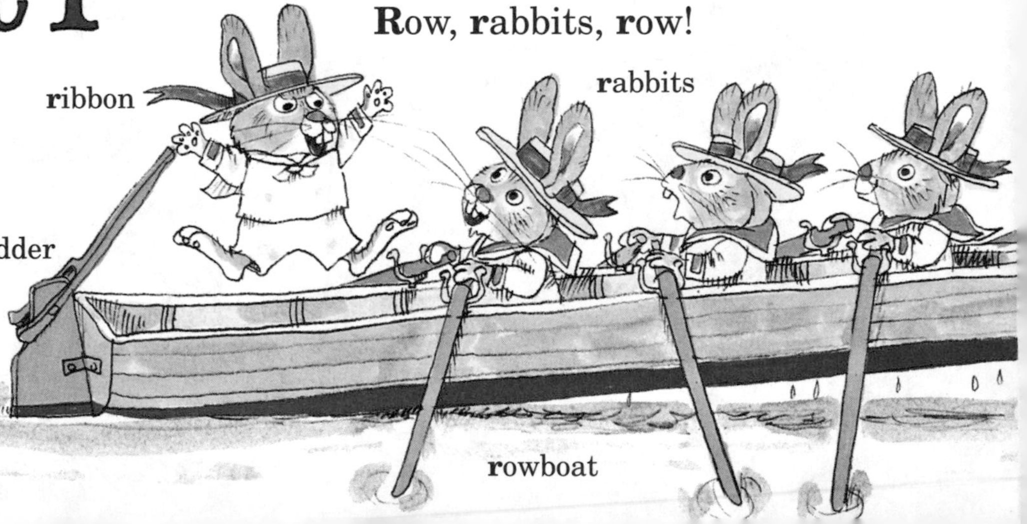

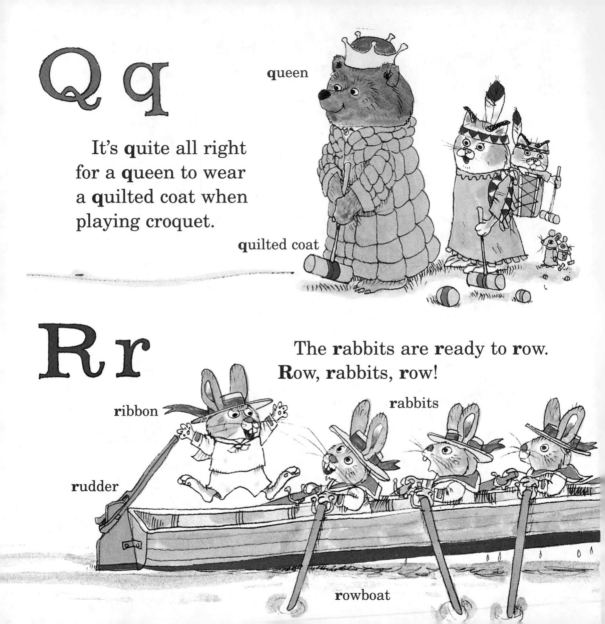

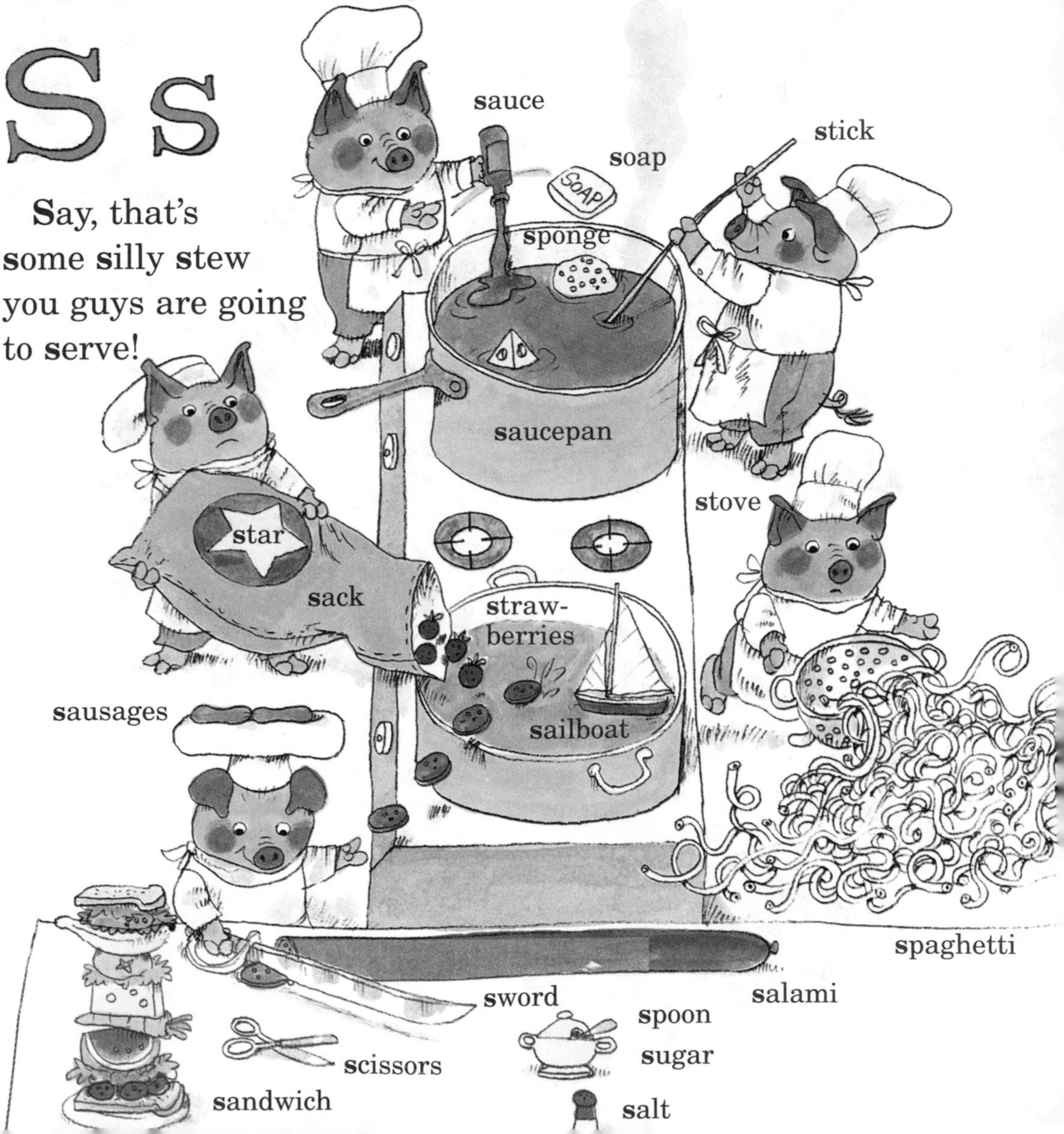

S s

Say, that's **s**ome **s**illy **s**tew you guys are going to **s**erve!

sauce

soap

sponge

stick

saucepan

stove

star

sack

strawberries

sailboat

sausages

spaghetti

sword

salami

spoon

scissors

sugar

sandwich

salt

T t

tomatoes

tires

train

track

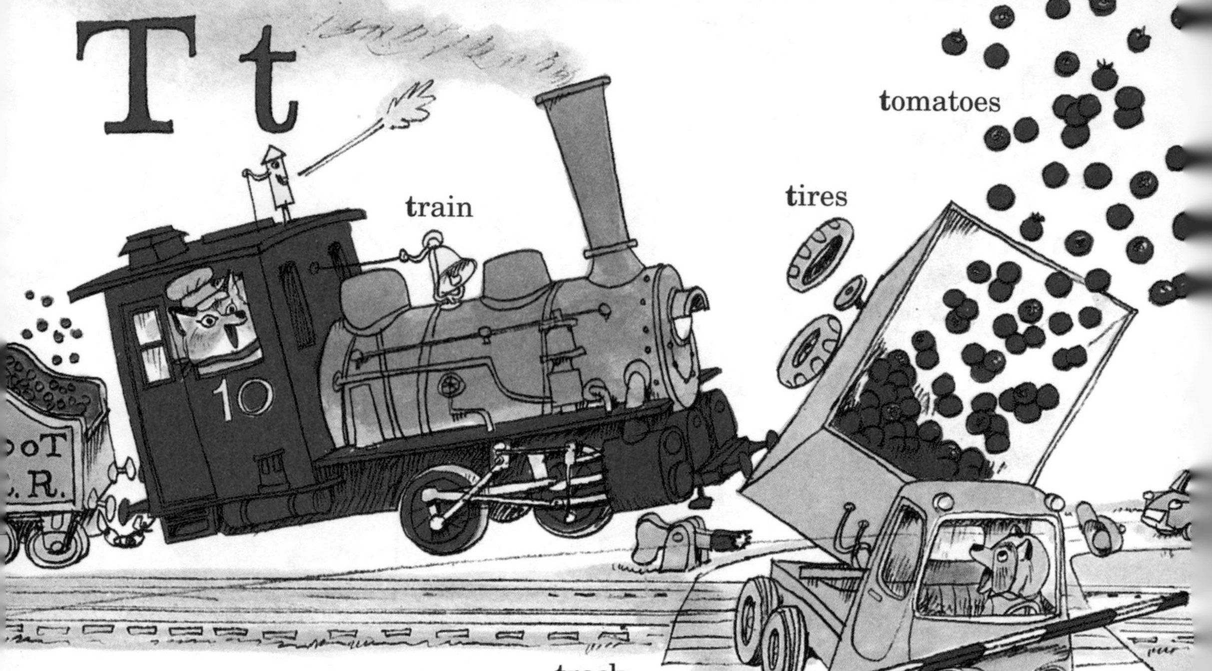

This is terrible!
The train is tumbling
into the tomato truck.

trailer truck

towel

tub

turtle

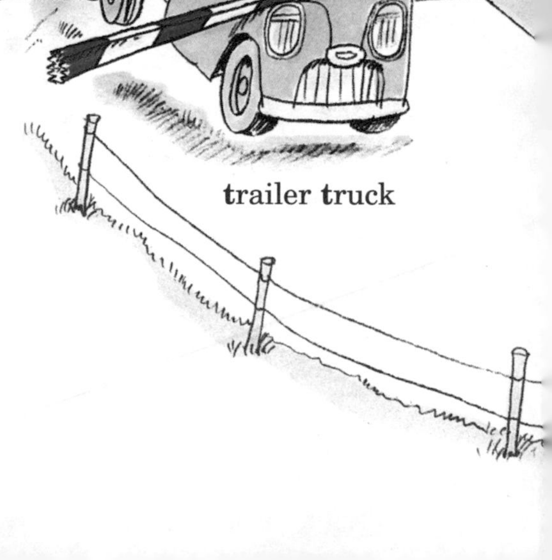

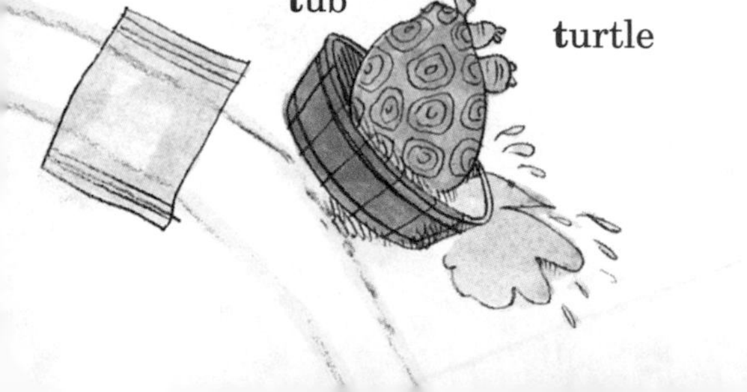

U u

umbrella

Unless you
want to get wet,
you'd better get
under the
umbrella, Lowly.

V v

Valentines
are a **v**ery
sweet gift on
Valentine's
Day.

valentine

W w

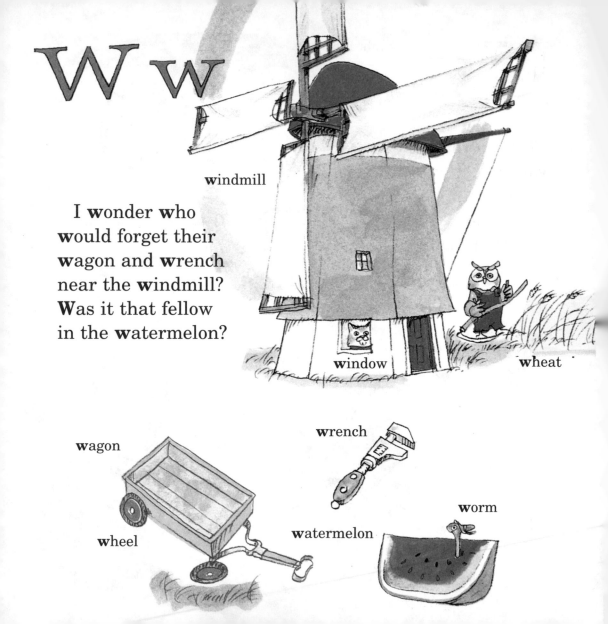

windmill

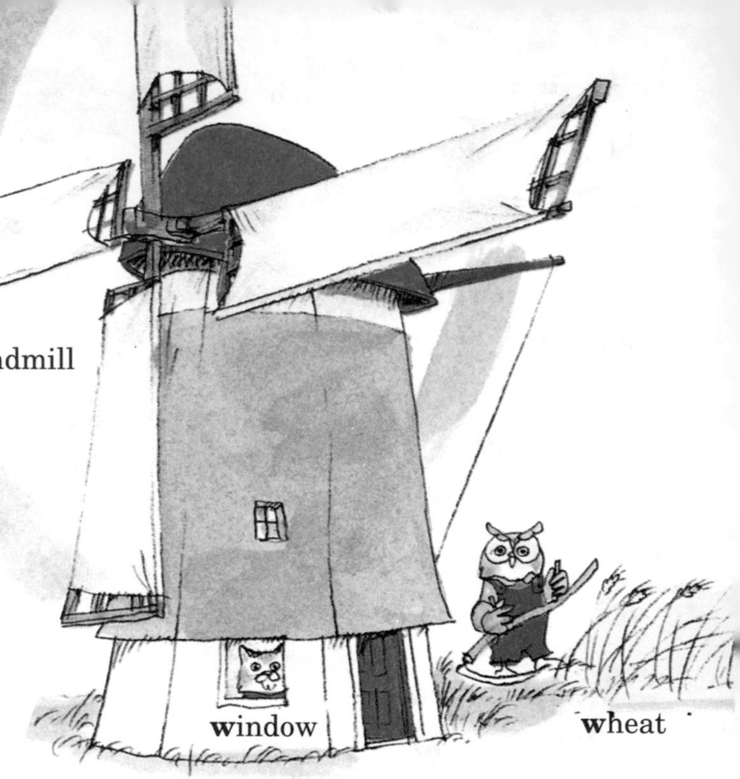

I **w**onder **w**ho **w**ould forget their **w**agon and **w**rench near the **w**indmill? **W**as it that fellow in the **w**atermelon?

window

wheat

wagon

wheel

wrench

watermelon

worm

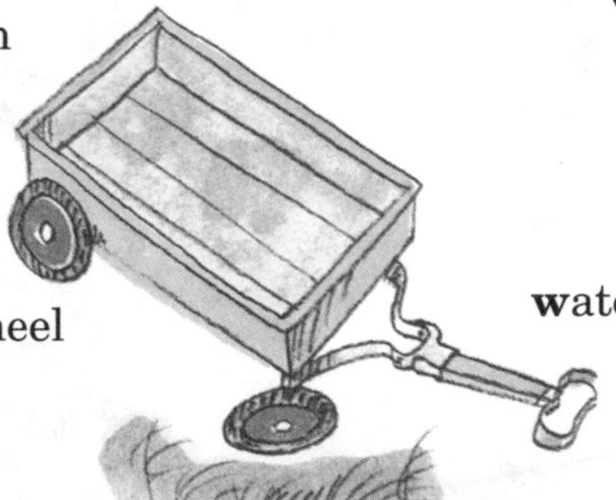

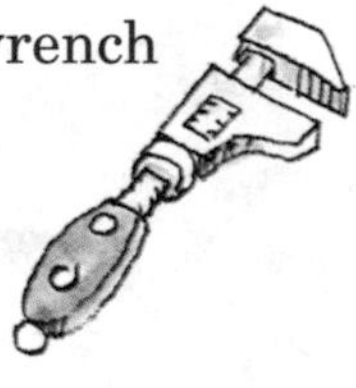

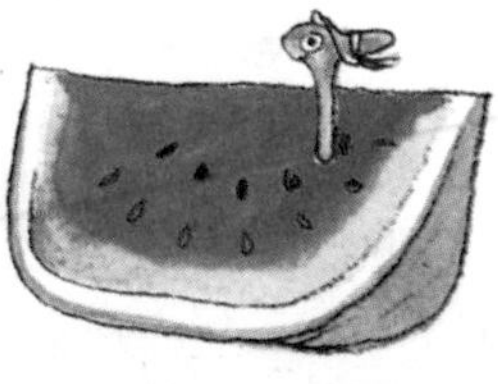

xylophone

Lowly Worm likes to play the **x**ylophone.

Y y

Why don't **y**ou share **y**our **y**o-yo with that **y**oung fellow, Mr. **Y**ak?

yak

yo-yo

Z z

Doesn't that **z**ebra look snazzy in his **z**ippered jacket?

zebra

zipper

Yellow stripes show the safe **z**one for crossing the street.

zone

zigzag

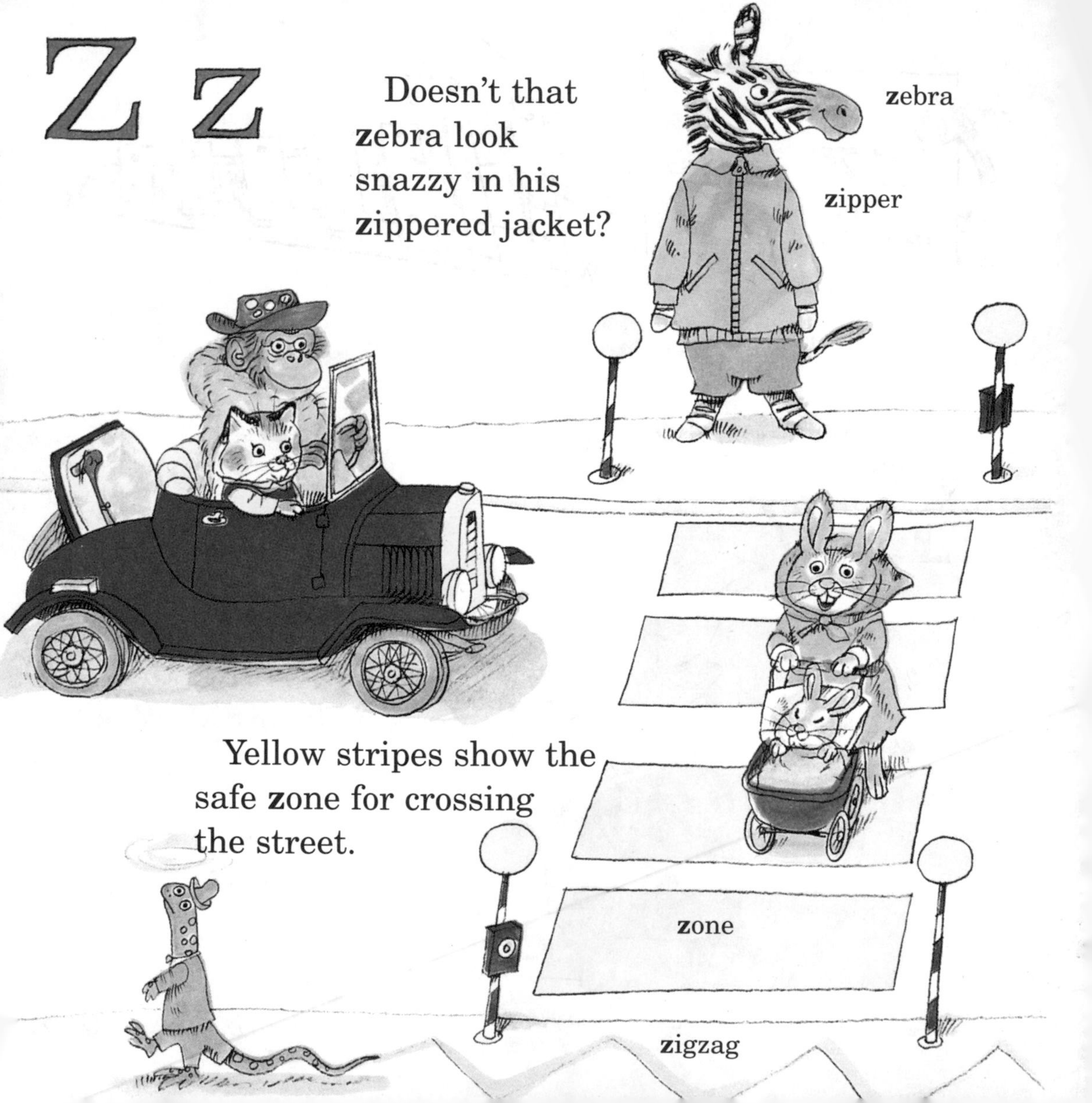